ISBN: 0692137866
ISBN 13: 9780692137864

Color Me Zombied Coloring Book

In a small town named Eidolon, a tragic accident happened that changed the people there forever. It was a long time ago now. There had been a secret project by the government to find a serum that would bring people back to life, and it worked, sort of. The people came back but they were mindless, meat craving zombies. Who knows what happened to those first test subjects but what happened to us is a story by itself.

No one in town knew about the tests or heard of them until the military was transporting the serum through our small town and the truck lost control and crashed. It exploded like a color-filled water balloon. The original plan had been to spread it over war zones so the scientists figured out how to turn it into a gas and when the truck exploded that's exactly what it did. The chemical turned into a cloud of smoke and moved through the town like as dense fog monster, changing all the people instead of healing them.

First they would fall over and start moaning. Then their feet would feel cold. When the unlucky people looked down, they would see their feet turning white and their clothes turning gray. Even the hair on their heads became white, gray or black.

Maybe they were zombies because of the lack of color, or maybe they could no longer see the colors since they were zombies but imagine the world without color. The town was now black, white and gray. No blues or reds, no purples, no color anywhere and without color, hope and inspiration vanished. A world without color was what everyone in Eidolon came to know, and soon colors were banned by the mayor.

Of course zombies need to eat meat or humans to survive and there weren't any humans around so initially they ate all the meat at the grocery stores but pretty soon they moved to the cemetery, which everyone agreed was gross. As they started to move out towards other towns they were met by an abundance of rodents to feed on and like cattle they mindlessly consumed the food they had in front of them. But where were all of these rodents coming from? Some say the military did this to keep the zombies away from civilians but who knows.

Once they ate enough meat from rats and squirrels , the town'speople began acting normal again, even though they were still zombies. But without colors, everyone in Eidolon lost the ability to smile or laugh. Some people thought the mayor was working with the government to cover up the tragedy, but it didn't matter. Colors were banned and no one asked questions. Eventually they came to fear colors. That is, until a zombie boy named Caleb made a discovery with the help of his dog, Max, and changed their world.

2

On a day like any other, Caleb was playing in the garage when Max came up with something in his mouth.

"You wanna play fetch, boy?" Caleb asked.

Max dropped a slobber-covered rat in front of Caleb and let out a loud WOOF!

"Mom's gonna be mad if she finds out we were playing with tomorrow's dinner," said Caleb.

Max wagged his tail and let out another impatient bark.

"Okay, okay, but if mom finds out, it's both of our butts," Caleb groaned.

Caleb grabbed the rat by the tail and flung it across the garage. It went further than he had intended and smashed into a bunch of rusty objects at the back of the garage, which came crashing down in a fit of noise.

"Oops! That's not good. We gotta find that rat before it's time for bed."

As Caleb and Max moved things out of the way, they began to notice something odd. There was a bright glow coming from under a pile of tools. Caleb moved what tools he could to get a better view.

"Whoooaaahh ..." said Caleb in amazement as color he had never seen before oozed from a spilled bucket of paint. This paint had not been affected by the chemical spill and had managed to stay hidden all these years. In fact, there were several buckets of paint sitting on the garage floor.

Caleb and Max stared at the color for a moment mesmerized. "Is this color?!" Caleb whispered to himself. His mind was racing with questions as he stared at the discovery.

He was just a toddler when everyone turned into zombies and had no memory of what colors looked like, but he had heard rumors and knew they were banned.

"Caleb, time for bed!" his mom yelled, startling him.

Caleb scooped the color back into the bucket in a hurry but noticed the other buckets filled with different colorful slime.

"I'm coming!" Caleb yelled as he put a few different colors into small containers he found, all while being careful not to touch the color with his skin.

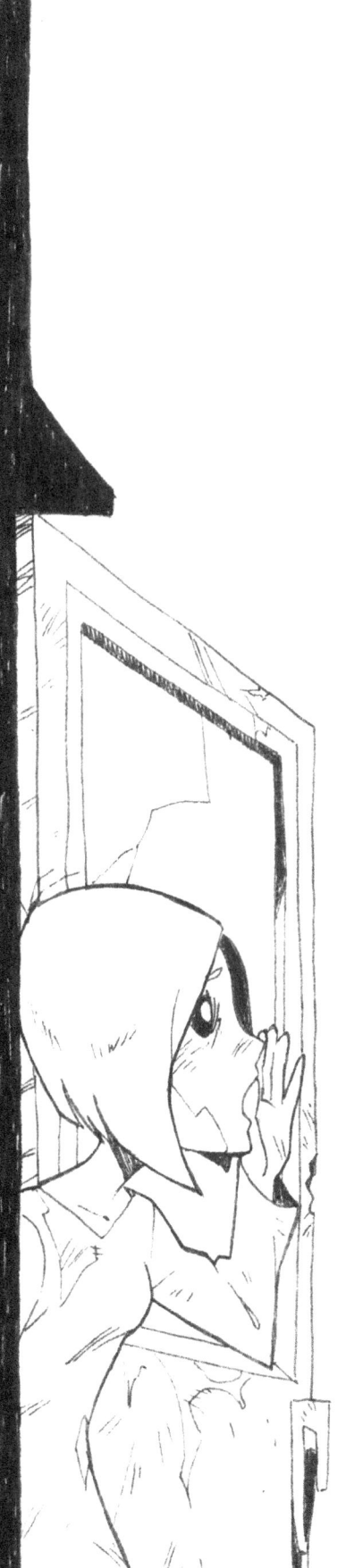

"I'm not going to say it again, young man, it's bed time!" cried Caleb's mom.

Caleb rushed to his room and hid the container in his backpack so his parents wouldn't see it.

"All right, son, hop in bed," Caleb's dad said as he entered the room with Caleb's mom. They tucked Caleb into bed and gave him a goodnight kiss.

"Goodnight, son. Don't forget to take something for show and tell tomorrow," said Caleb's mom. "Maybe you could bring one of your stuffed animals? I haven't seen you play with Neko in a while."

"I can't find him. He's lost, remember mom? Don't worry, though, I have something special to bring," Caleb said as he turned over and fell asleep.

That night Caleb dreamed of the colors he had discovered, and something happened for the first time since the chemical spill: a smile came across his sleeping face.

The next day at school, Caleb's teacher, Ms. Alexander, instructed the class on what was expected of them for show and tell.

"All right, students. It's show and tell today, so if you have something you would like to share with the class, please raise your hand and come up to the front when you are called on."

Caleb sat with the containers of colors in his backpack, ready to present them to the class. He was the first one to raise his hand.

"Come up to the front, Caleb," Ms. Alexander said, "and share what you brought." Caleb walked up to the front with his backpack and said, "I have something special I found in my garage."

Caleb slowly pulled out the container of colors and opened it. All the students let out a loud gasp!

Caleb's teacher, on the other hand, was horrified.

"Caleb! Put that away! Right now!" yelled Ms. Alexander.

Caleb put the colors away quickly, and the other kids stared in confusion as Ms. Alexander rushed Caleb to the principal's office.

Caleb's parents were called down to the school to speak with the principal, Mr. Mosburg.

10

"Your son was caught with colored paint in class today," the principal explained. "I hope this is not something allowed at your house, and I would recommend disciplining your son before it is too late."

"No one has had any contact with color in years. I would hope this situation gets taken care of and no one else has to hear about it. We all know how angry the mayor would get, and the consequences are not something I care to imagine." The principal paused for a moment with a look of confusion. This was the first time the word "imagine" had been spoken since they all became zombies.

"I'm sorry, I don't know where that came from ... As I was saying, colors are forbidden, you know this. This will not leave the office, and I will be speaking with the other students."

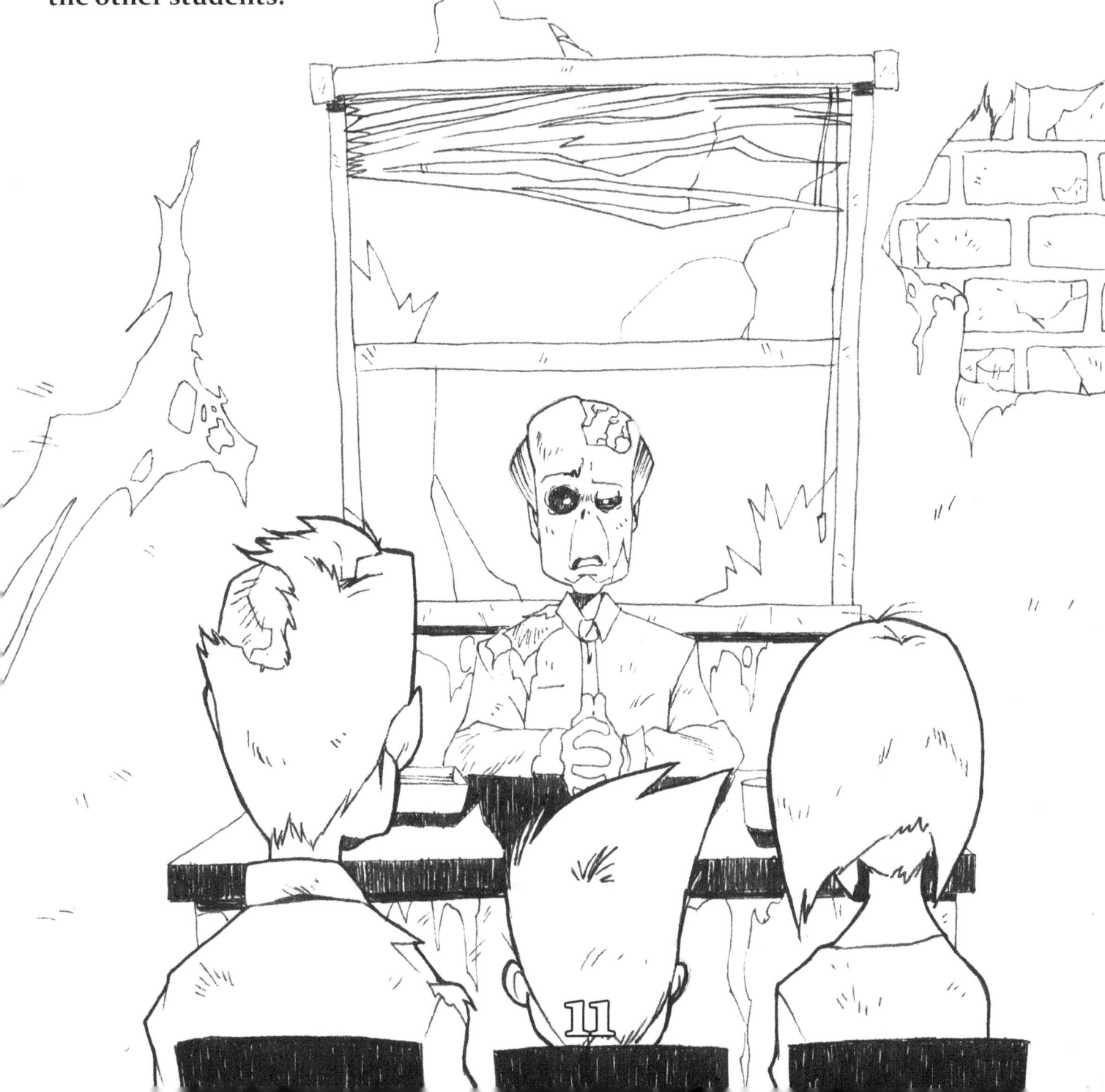

Caleb and his parents left the principal's office with a warning. The car ride home was quiet, and Caleb sat in the back wondering what he had done wrong.

"Mom, Dad, I don't understand why I got in trouble. Colors are beautiful. Why are they not allowed anymore?" asked Caleb.

"The world is black and white now, son. Sometimes it's just best to leave things the way they are," replied Caleb's dad. "Did you find that paint in the garage?"

"Yes sir," Caleb replied.

"I'll get the cans tomorrow and inform the military so they can get rid of them," said Caleb's dad.

The rest of the car ride home was silent. Caleb stared out the car window, still wondering why colors were not allowed.

13

Caleb's parents tucked him into bed that night promising tomorrow would be better. His parents seemed to melt away as he got lost in his thoughts. They kissed him goodnight and turned out the lights. Caleb lay in silence trying to understand how colors could be bad when they were so beautiful.

He sat in the darkness of his room and looked around at how plain it seemed now. He let out a sigh as he slowly closed his eyes. He tried to push colors out of his mind, but the more he tried not to think about them, the brighter they appeared. When he opened his eyes, his room was covered in swirls of color. Something changed right then as Caleb used his imagination for the first time and like a bolt of lightning striking a kite, he knew what he had to do to make tomorrow a much brighter day.

15

Caleb lay in silence until he knew his parents were asleep and then quietly got out of bed and motioned for Max to follow him.

"I'll color the whole town, and then everyone will see how amazing colors are," Caleb said to himself. "Come on, Max. I'm going to need your help!"

Caleb and Max snuck out to the garage and grabbed as many paint buckets as they could and put them into his wagon. Looking at the cans of paint, Caleb could see faded images of people using brushes to paint things. He quickly looked around the garage in hopes he might find some. Luckily he found a couple underneath some rusted tools.

17

With his wagon full, Caleb started walking down the street. He began coloring everything he could from flowers to cars, houses and fences. He colored fire hydrants green and bushes blue, houses orange and purple, too. No matter what it was, Caleb colored it and used as many colors as he could. The town began to transform right before his eyes. All of the black and white was soon replaced with radiant colors.

18

After a full night of coloring, Caleb and Max went back home to bed as the sun started to rise. They both crawled into bed, exhausted, and fell fast asleep.

The next morning, everyone was shocked as they stepped outside to see the town full of color. The kids were thrilled with what they saw, but their parents were upset and scared.

The townsfolk gathered outside the town hall to hear the mayor and to voice their frustrations.

"Now, everyone, I know you're all concerned, but I assure you we are working as fast as we can to take care of this situation," said the mayor.

Parents yelled back in anger. "This will not stand!" cried one parent. "What about the children?" screamed another. "We want answers!"

"CALEB!" The sound of his name being yelled startled him. "CALEB, GET DOWN HERE RIGHT NOW!" his mom shouted.

Caleb jumped out of bed and ran downstairs into the kitchen. Half asleep, he forgot he was covered in paint. As he turned the corner, Caleb's parents let out a gasp.

"We know what you've done, young man, you're covered in paint! Everyone in town is furious. You're the only one who has used colors since they were banned. What do you have to say for yourself?" asked Caleb's dad. Caleb stood in silence, looking at the ground.

"Let us see your hands," said Caleb's mom sternly. She was still hoping he was not to blame, knowing full well that wasn't possible. Caleb slowly brought his hands forward. They were covered in paint. "Oh, son, this is not good. Why would you do this?" asked Caleb's mom. Caleb was silent.

"We're going to the town hall so you can apologize," said Caleb's dad. They got in the car and passed all the colorful things Caleb had painted in the night. The colors melted into a large, bright blur as Caleb sank down into the back seat, afraid of what was going to happen.

23

When they reached the town hall, everyone was still yelling and demanding answers. Caleb's parents led him to the podium as the mayor told everyone the person to blame for the colors had something to say. Caleb stood up before the townspeople as silence fell over the crowd. They were shocked that the small boy standing before them was the one who colored the town.

Caleb looked at his parents and Max one last time before he spoke. "I'm sorry for coloring everything," Caleb said in a quiet voice. "I was only trying to show everyone how beautiful colors can make the world." The adults erupted in anger.

"Why would you do such a thing? Colors are not beautiful. They make things messy," someone cried. Caleb was frightened and sad. A tear rolled down his face and as he wiped it away, the colors on his hand rubbed off on his cheek.

In this moment of great fear and sadness for Caleb, a group of voices yelled from the back of the crowd, "We like the colors!"

25

Everyone turned around and looked in astonishment at the group of kids standing before them.

"We think the colors are beautiful. We should be thanking Caleb" said one small girl. "Can't you see how much better our town is now? You have to understand!" exclaimed another child.

All the children went and stood next to Caleb. The grownups stood in awe and didn't know what to say. They also noticed the kids were all smiling for the first time since they became zombies. Caleb's parents now understood what Caleb was doing as the children all gathered together. They saw the colors as something to admire and embrace. Colors had the power to bring everyone together. Caleb's parents now joined him and the crowd of children as Caleb's dad picked him up and put him on his shoulders.

"We know what our son did seems horrible, but seeing these kids shows us how special colors are and makes me remember how joyful things used to be before this whole mess," said Caleb's dad with a smile.

Caleb's mom turned to him. "We're sorry, son. We should have listened to you. Colors are beautiful!" she said with a smile.

All the grownups looked at each other and then at the children, and just like the chemical had spread through the town turning them into zombies, smiles spread through the crowd. The anger they felt melted away as they understood how special colors were to the children. The crowd erupted with laughter and joy as the families hugged each other.

The crowd walked through the town to enjoy the colors. Caleb was on his dad's shoulders at the front of the crowd. Everyone spent the rest of the day looking at the many colors that now made their town beautiful, while smiling and laughing. Something else also changed as the sky regained its color; or rather, they saw what had been there all along but they had been unable to see.

Even though no one believed him, Caleb inspired and change the world, simply by believing in himself. But this was only the beginning. The town decided to get together every year to celebrate the day they were brought back to life by color. So always remember that even when other people don't believe in you, hold true to who you are and help create a world bright and full of color, just as Caleb did.

29

30